H

HEALING HEARTS

A Stormy Love Story

Sophie Thurn

HEALING HEARTS

eBook ISBN-13: 978-1-64953-933-5
Paperback ISBN-13: 978-1-64953-932-8
Audiobook ISBN-13: 978-1-64953-935-9

CONTENTS

HEALING HEARTS

ABOUT THE BOOK

HEALING HEARTS: A STORMY LOVE STORY

In the heart of the Hamptons, amidst the luxurious houses and lifestyles of the ultra-rich two souls collide in a passionate and redemptive romance.

Dr. Alexander Knight, a billionaire doctor to the stars exuding dominant charisma, has always commanded control over his life—until he encounters Emma Lowe. Emma, a brilliant and resilient single mother and flight nurse is determined to break free from a toxic past and forge a brighter future for her daughter, Lily.

Their worlds collide in a swirling hurricane, creating a connection that neither can resist. As Emma worries about the storm , she finds herself irresistibly drawn to the magnetic Dr. Knight. Boundaries blur, professionalism wavers, and love blossoms amidst the pounding rain and punishing winds that could tear them apart.

Yet, with Emma's haunting past and Alexander's commitment to non-commitment, can their burgeoning romance withstand the complexities of their lives? Will love conquer all, or will their worlds collide, leaving them shattered once more?

In "Healing Hearts: A Stormy Love Story," passion, resilience, and the irresistible force of love converge in a tale of second chances. Join

Emma and Dr. Knight as they navigate a path of healing, trust, and the promise of a happily ever after.

CHAPTER 1

ALEXANDER

The blades of the helicopter slow, the steady *whump* changing from a roar to a dull heartbeat as I exit the chopper and walk back to the office. I'm exhausted; I've been up for nearly twenty-four hours, flying all over the coast, trying to keep up with the demands of my very particular patients.

Being a house call doctor in one of the wealthiest zip codes in the United States, my clients are demanding. They have high standards, and they won't take no for an answer.

It's a good thing that I'm just as much of an asshole as they are, or I wouldn't be nearly as successful as I am.

It's a beautiful late summer day in the Hamptons, and I flip my sunglasses over my eyes to block the brilliant rays of the setting sun. There's a huge wall of clouds off to the east, which is some kind of storm that's been on the news for days, but I haven't paid attention to until today.

Luckily, I'm done with calls for the night, so we can hunker down until it's done.

I don't necessarily love the scenery; it's just part of my job. Part of the empire I've built, choosing to maintain the health and well-being of the ultra-rich so that I can take some of the fortune they have and put it

3

in my own pocket. So many of my colleagues in medical school wanted to get into being a doctor to help people, to save people. To make the world a better place.

That's great for them.

I wanted to get rich, and I've done a pretty damn good job of that.

"Dr. Knight!" a voice calls. I glance at the door and see my assistant, Erika, as she waves to me from the office door.

I stride up to the door, my white coat snapping in the breeze from the helicopter's blades.

"How was Mr. Worth?" Erika asks politely.

I shrug. "Alive. Definitely not having a heart attack, despite his best efforts to convince me."

She giggles, and the sound grates on my nerves.

I hired Erika because she was hot as hell, and that hasn't changed. However, after we hooked up a while ago, she's been fawning over me a little too much, and it's getting annoying. I brush past her, opening the door to the main office building.

Inside, there's a familiar face behind the main desk.

I frown.

It's my new flight nurse, Emma.

New is a relative term. I hired Emma because of her background. Like me, she's former military; I was Army, she was Air Force. I know nothing about her other than she's an exceptional flight nurse.

And she's the bane of my existence.

I'm used to women giving me whatever I want. I smile, they melt. I flash my eyes at them, they fall over. It's practically part of the fiber of my being at this point, and it makes my life pretty darn easy.

This rule applies to everyone, it seems, except Emma Lowe.

"Emma," I grit my teeth as I nod at her. If she wasn't so goddamn good at what she did, I'd fire her.

A very small part of me protests, and states that the fact she doesn't fall all over herself for me isn't a valid reason to fire her.

I squash it quickly.

Emma's smile falls, and she folds her arms. She glares back at me. "Dr. Knight."

She hasn't once used my name.

I, of course, go by Dr. Knight. My whole brand is built around it. I didn't do two tours in Iraq and go to metical school just to go by "Alexander", after all. But again, normally women will get bold and try to use my given name at some point.

Emma has never once tried.

It's another reminder of the professional boundary she set between us. Should I be happy about that boundary? Absolutely. It means that Emma is competent in a way that's rare.

It's also irritating as hell.

"Did you update Mr. Worth's chart?" she scans my distinct lack of paperwork with a scathing glance.

I'm too tired for this, and I am absolutely not going to take the time to update a chart right now. Instead, I do something that is a dick move, even for me. I shake my head and toss my phone at her. "Notes are in there."

Her eyes narrow and spark with irritation. "You want me to just … transcribe your notes for you?"

I resist the urge to cringe, committing to the words, and I nod instead. "Yes. I do."

Vaguely, I'm aware that I'm being a total jerk. I can see Emma's cheeks redden and I know she's about ten seconds from becoming totally enraged.

I should back off.

But some dark part of me loves her emotional reactions. Normally she's cool as a cucumber, so I do occasionally provoke her just to see her reaction. When I get to see her angry, it's…

It's kind of sexy.

She hisses and tosses the phone back at me. "Update the notes before you fly out again."

I catch the phone, and she storms away.

Inside, I'm practically cackling with glee. I might have had a terrible night but seeing Emma Lowe get flustered makes everything worth it.

I open the door to my office and sit at my desk. I heave a sigh, leaning back in my office chair. My eyes close, and I pinch the bridge of my nose with my fingers.

God, I'm tired.

I'm about to fall asleep when I hear a timid knock at the door. "Come in," I call.

Erika slips into the room. "Jackson Hart just called."

I'm awake in an instant. Jackson Hart, CEO of the biggest music conglomerate in the world, is one of the clients I've been after for ages.

If he's calling me, this could be it. It could be my chance, finally.

"What did he say?"

She checks her notes. "He asked you and a nurse to be ready at his house. He and his wife are flying back from London, and he wants you to be on hand when they arrive."

"Did he say why?"

"She's six months pregnant and wasn't feeling well," Erika smiles. "Aw, that's so sweet."

There's nothing sweet about it. Pregnancy is one of the most complicated human conditions, and it's amazing to me every time that babies are successfully born. "Did he say anything else?"

She shakes her head. "Nope. Just to bring your best nurse and meet him there."

"Who's on the schedule today?"

My eyes drift to the schedule we have at the same time.

My heart sinks when I see the only nurse on duty.

Fuck.

"Any idea how long it's going to take them to fly back from London?"

Erika shrugs. "Once they leave it's a five-hour flight so..." her voice trails off.

I grit my teeth.

I already knew that. I have the flight times to the nearest ten major cities memorized. My eyes drift to the news, where the newscaster is pointing aggressively

If they haven't even left yet, we could be waiting for a while.

The last thing I want to do is be stuck with Emma Lowe for an extended period of time.

I sigh. "Get Emma ready. She's coming with me."

CHAPTER 2

EMMA

Nervously, I check my phone. I'm praying that my mom can watch Lily while I'm out on this call. If not, I'm totally screwed. Her school is out for summer, and that's not even the best option considering the circumstances. With the storm rolling in, I have no idea how long we're going to be out on this one.

Dr. Knight, once again, is testing my patience by making stupid moves.

I get it.

I respect that he's done such a great job of building up his business. Knight Consulting, his medical company, has exploded in the last ten years. He has branches all across the country; LA, Sun Valley, Aspen, Taos, Chicago... anywhere there's rich people, there's a branch of the business, each helicopter branded with a tasteful silver logo. I glance at that logo now as we hop onto the chopper, ducking low so the propeller blades above don't take us out.

I'm short enough that it's probably never going to be an issue, but my military training takes over in moments like this. Also, "I'm probably never going to be chopped by a helicopter blade" is not quite safe enough for my tastes.

I pull myself into the door, then close it and settle in. Dr. Knight has done a fantastic job of making every aspect of his clinic something that can be marketed, packaged, and profited upon. The helicopter is as luxurious as they come, in order to appeal to his target market. There's top-of-the line medical equipment, leather seats, and even charging ports for cell phones. It's a far cry from the UH-60 that I used to fly on in the Air Force, but I can't say that I miss those old rust buckets.

This one is like flying around in a Rolls-Royce, and I love it.

It's unfortunate that I have to share the helicopter with Dr. Knight.

I wish I could say that I've met a more arrogant man, but it's unfortunately untrue. I think that if there was an Olympic medal for overall alpha-asshole-ness, my ex-husband and Dr. Knight would probably fight over the title every year.

Generally, Troy Ververs, my ex, would win, but only because he turned out to be both a shitty husband and a terrible father, and a stalker to boot.

Dr. Knight has no kids and, to my knowledge, has never been married, so it could be he just hasn't had the opportunity to totally screw those two things up yet.

Honestly, anything is possible when it comes to him. He's limitless, in more ways than one. His persistence and dedication to his job knows no boundaries.

Unfortunately, neither does his ego.

He's exactly the type of insufferable alpha male that I would have fallen head over heels for... ten years ago.

Now, at twenty-eight, I know better. I've got the divorce papers and the kid to prove it. I've grown up, and one of my hard-earned life lessons is that I have to avoid people like Dr. Alexander Knight at all costs.

Working for him might not have been the best idea, sure. But the pay is good. Okay, it's better than good... with this salary, I'm able to put my kid in a private school that makes a future possible for her that I never would have dreamed of for myself. She's in a kindergarten class with kids who are related to Kennedys.

It's a long way from the trailer park I grew up in, and I'm so excited for her.

The pay is worth it, sure.

Until I have to actually interact with Dr. Knight.

Somehow, he's always able to find my weaknesses and exploit them. It doesn't matter what it is; Dr. Knight finds a way to piss me off, no matter what.

Even now, just sitting in the helicopter, he's annoying.

No man has a right to be that handsome.

He's sprawled out in the pilot's seat, his aviator glasses on despite the dark skies. Under those dark shades, he's got sea-green eyes, which turn darker when he's mad. I've never seen him happy, but I assume they do the opposite when he is. He's tall, so tall that I'm actually kind of surprised they tracked him into pilot school. He somehow ended up as both pilot and doctor after leaving the Army, both of which require a hell of a lot more time put in to be legit in the civilian world. I've googled him before; he's about ten years older than I am, so it makes sense to me that he had the time to dedicate to both careers.

What doesn't make sense is how ridiculously attractive he looks while doing it.

Pipe down, Emma, I whisper to myself mentally.

Dr. Knight is attractive. Absolutely.

But all that sexiness comes at a cost, and it's one that I'm definitely never going to be willing to pay.

CHAPTER 3

ALEXANDER

By the time we land at the Hart estate, there's more than just a couple of storm clouds gathering. The wind is whipping overhead, and even though I'm a damn good pilot, my heart beats a little louder than normal as I struggle to land the luxury helicopter.

A couple of times, I glance over at Emma.

Her face is pale, and she's got a death grip on a safety handle, but she doesn't complain. She doesn't even give any indication that she's afraid of the storm. I'm not even sure I see her flinch; despite the fact she's holding on to the handle with an iron grip.

Nope. No flinching. Not once.

I'm kind of flattered. She either trusts me completely, or she's used to stressful situations.

Weirdly, I hope that she trusts me.

Logically, I know that she probably just is used to situations like this. I know from her Air Force experience that she was a combat medic, just like I was.

As I started to turn the rotor off, I wondered why she chose to get a flight nurse certification after her military service, instead of pursuing the full doctor degree.

I open my mouth to ask, but a slice of lightning streaks across the sky, followed by a crack of thunder so loud, the glass in the helicopter's windshield shakes.

"Let's get inside," I shout to Emma.

She nods and wordlessly follows me.

The helipad is on the Hart grounds. Along with many other ultra-rich clients, the Harts have more than just a house out here in the Hamptons. They have a compound. Theirs includes a helipad, several guest houses that they rent out to less wealthy friends, and of course the main house.

Part of my instructions include directions to get into the pool house. I sprint for it, glancing back over my shoulder to see if Emma is behind me. The rain is absolutely slamming into us now; giant sheets of water that ride the wind to rasp against our faces. I grit my teeth; the water is cold as ice.

This doesn't feel like a regular summer storm, and apprehension builds in my heart.

This feels like a hurricane.

I rack my brain to try and remember if the news had said anything about the h-word, but I honestly can't remember. All I can remember is thinking about Emma, and how vividly annoyed she was going to be at having to come with me on this trip.

And, honestly, being a little thrilled about it.

I punch the code to the lock into the guest house door. "Guest house" is a loose term… this house is bigger than what most people in America ever dream of owning. The door opens, and Emma and I fall inside. I deactivate the lock and send Hart and his wife a quick text letting them know we've arrived.

Hart: *Good. Thanks for that.*

Knight: *Welcome. How's it looking for your ETA?*

Hart: *Well, considering the storm just got upgraded to a Category 2, probably not for a while. They won't let us out of London until it clears.*

I sigh. I was worried about that.

Knight: 10-4. *Let us know when you're on the way. Wife good?*

I mean medically, but he sends me a picture. It's a selfie of both of them. Hart, I know. He's also ex-military, Navy, and I've been trying to court him for quite some time now. The wife is new to me. She's beautiful; visibly extremely pregnant, but her arms are wrapped around him, and despite the shadows on her face, she looks chipper.

Something strange inside of me twinges at the sight of them.

I don't respond to the picture. I'm not one to linger on sentimental stuff, nor am I going to consider what it is inside of me that seems to be a little too interested in the closeness they have in that picture.

That life is never for me.

I made sure of that a long time ago.

I blow out a breath and check my aviation weather app. A dozen warnings, alarms, and bolded red words convey that I'm right.

This is a hurricane now.

Shit. I'll have to pay Emma overtime. We're going to be here for a while longer than the five-hour flight from London.

Not that it really matters. My company is on the top of the world; I can afford to pay Emma nearly double what she's making now.

Hell. Triple, if I felt so inclined.

I give her an appraising look. She's standing in the entryway, her helmet still on, dripping from the edges of her flight suit. Her overnight back is in a soggy puddle on the floor. I'm sure mine isn't in much better shape, but hers looks… sad. She looks firm in contrast to the flaccid bag; I can picture her receiving orders or embarking on a mission with that same expression.

She looks tough.

Maybe I should give her a raise. She's a damn good flight nurse; the best I've ever hired, actually. She's smart and competent, and she frequently has insights about our work that I begrudgingly turn into reality, because they're damn good. If I we could stand each other for more than ten seconds, I actually think we'd make pretty good teammates.

But if wishes were fishes everyone would eat.

I wave my phone. "They're stuck in London. Storm's a Cat 2 now. We're stuck here for a while."

For the first time, I see a fissure of fear cross her face. "I see."

That's what she has a reaction to? "Don't worry," I snip. "I'll pay you overtime."

Her fear twists, changing to anger. "Do you think that's what I'm worried about?"

"What else?"

She folds her arms and cocks out a hip. "Some of us have other obligations, you know. I have a life outside of my work."

Suddenly, I'm absolutely burning to know what that life is. "Oh? Did you have a hot date scheduled?"

The image of her, dressed up, out on a date in the city, makes an appearance in my mind. She'd look phenomenal in a short black dress. Some kind of sexy shoes. Taking my hand as we…

Wait a minute.

My hand?

Nope. If she's on a date, it's not with me. It's with someone else. I try to fix the image in my mind, but the second I picture another man in my place, my frustration warps into something else.

Rage.

"If I did, it would literally be none of your business," she snaps.

"I definitely think it's my business who my employees date," I snort.

Her eyes blink like she can't believe what I've said, and I see her cheeks turn red. "Excuse me? Are you fucking kidding?"

"No," I say coolly back. Part of me is desperate to backpedal, to explain. To just stop running my mouth.

Unfortunately, I've never been very good at going back.

Only forward.

Before she can explode into a torrent of what I'm sure is a well-deserved tongue-lashing, I hold up a hand. "Never mind. We're stuck here through the storm. Get changed, I'll get us something to eat."

I leave her there, fuming in the entryway, and I go to find a room I can change in.

And I try, to the best of my ability, to get the image of Emma and me out on a date out of my mind.

CHAPTER 4

EMMA

Alexander Knight is literally the worst human being I've ever met. And I'm stuck here, in some rich guy's house, with him. Until a hurricane chooses to make its merry way back out into the ocean.

I'm fuming as I unpack the soggy contents of my bag. For some reason, the morning when I packed it, I grabbed the least durable bag I own. I had been meaning to swap it out for weeks now, but every time I got close, I got distracted or forgot.

I'm regretting it now as I wring out my soaking extra clothes.

They're nothing fancy. Just some black yoga pants and a comfortable black shirt. Some serviceable underwear. Just an extra set of clothes to wear in case of an event like this.

An event like this, however, seems like much bigger of a deal now than it was when I packed the back.

I text my mom, but it seems like she's okay. She and Lily are snuggled in for the night, safely tucked into my childhood home in New Haven. Mom confirms that the storm is kicking up there as well, but I'm confident it's worse here.

The Hamptons are, after all, on a freaking barrier island.

For the thousandth time, I curse under my breath. I can't believe I'm stuck here with Dr. Knight.

I hope the storm blows through quickly.

I check my phone; I have less than 20% battery left. I rifle through some of the drawers in the guest room I'm in, and I find a charger. I plug it into the wall, grateful that rich people just leave stuff wherever they go.

After a hot shower, I'm feeling marginally better. I can appreciate my surroundings... the bathroom is a vision in marble and gilded features, and the rain shower and expensive shampoo I find there does wonders on my mood.

I'm drying my hair, dressed in my somewhat moist extra outfit, when the power goes out.

I curse again, and grope for my phone in the dark. Turning the flashlight on, I stumble back into the hallway. The small pool of light from my phone seems tiny against the fierce power of the storm.

I follow it anyway.

"Dr. Knight?" I call out. I hate how my voice sounds so small in the darkness. I'm a combat veteran, a single mom, and the survivor of a hellacious divorce. I'm definitely not a little girl afraid of the dark.

But I would like to know where the hell my boss is.

"In here," he responds, his voice coming from the kitchen.

I shiver.

His voice is sexy, of course. Just like everything else about him, I guess.

I walk into the kitchen, where a warm glow prompts me to turn my phone light off.

Somehow, he managed to find candles.

And wine, if the two glasses filled with dark liquid are what I think they are.

Knowing Dr. Knight, there's an equal chance that they could be the blood of his enemies, but there is a fancy-looking bottle there as well, so I'm going to assume wine.

He gestures to two packages on the table. "Looks like their chef left them some options."

I walk into the room, leaning my elbows on the marble counter-top. There's some kind of French-sounding chicken, and beef wellington.

I raise my eyebrow back at Dr. Knight. "What's your preference?"

He shrugs. "I'm easy. Whatever you don't want."

I snort. Dr. Knight and "easy" aren't even in the same universe.

Let alone sentence.

I grab the chicken, rip it open, and stare. "No microwave, huh?"

He laughs. "Shit. I forgot about that."

His laugh seems to skate over my skin. I toss the frozen meal down and reach for the wine.

Dr. Knight watches, his eyes shimmering in the dark. "I hope you like red."

I shrug. "Wine is wine."

"Anyone who says that hasn't had truly good wine."

"Oh, for the love," I snap, the edge of the glass at my lips. "You can be so…"

"Accurate?"

"Snobby," I finish. I'm tired, cold, and I'm worried about my kid. There's a literal hurricane outside beating down on this house, and I've had enough of Dr. Knight's bullshit.

So, instead of even trying to be professional, I lift the glass up in a toast. "To you, the king of pretentious assholes," I say.

I don't wait for his reaction.

I drink the wine.

He's silent, even after my barb. I take a huge gulp before I muster the courage to look back at him.

His eyes are almost predatory in the candlelight, and a shiver of arousal moves over my body.

"Is that what you think I am, Emma?"

I know he's said my name before.

I'm sure of it.

But the context was different.

Here, in the dark, with the rain clawing at the windows of some-one's amazing guest house, the context is…

He shouldn't say my name like that.

I take another huge gulp of wine. "I think you're more than that, Dr. Knight," I retort.

It appears that the combination of frustration and (admittedly very good) wine has given my tongue a life of its own.

But I'm not about to back down now.

"Alexander," he says in a low voice.

I stop, mid-gulp, and lower my glass. "What?"

I watch him grab the other glass of wine, lifting it to his lips. I watch the smooth column of his throat work as he drinks. When he pulls the glass away, his tongue darts out to collect any stray drops of liquid, and my heart skips a beat.

"Alexander," he repeats.

I shake my head. "I don't understand."

"Emma. We're stuck together in a hurricane. We are having wine for dinner. For the love of God, stop calling me Dr. Knight. Call me Alexander."

"No," I say quickly. I drain the rest of my glass and reach for the bottle to pour more.

He watches my movements with dark eyes. "Why not?"

"Why do you care?" I take another sip. I can feel the wine affecting me now; my fingers and lips have the familiar buzz that lets me know I'm getting a little tipsy.

I put the bottle back. This will be my last glass.

I don't trust myself to have another.

He frowns. "I care because I'm your employer."

"And I address you as such."

"Even when the situation is this informal?" he gestures to the surroundings.

I gulp. "Especially when the situation is this informal."

It's meant to state that there's a boundary between us. I need to keep this professional; I need to keep him at arm's length. I need to keep Dr. Alexander Knight in the tight, neat box I've built for him.

Because if I let him out, I'm afraid of what's going to happen.

His eyes glint, and I have the distinct impression that he's somehow spotted a weakness in what I said.

"I see." He sips again. His long fingers play with the delicate stem of the glass, and I can't help but stare at them when he puts the wine down.

"I want to hear you say my name, Emma."

I bark out a laugh. "Make me."

I know, instantly, that it's the wrong thing to say.

He leans forward. The counter is large, but the second he moves, the safe amount of space between us disappears.

I can feel the heat radiating off of his body. This house is cold, and I want to arch into it like a cat.

His lips are curled into a mischievous smile. His eyes glitter, like he's some kind of trickster god.

"And how, Emma, can I make you say my name?"

"Your guess is as good as mine," I snap. I want to retreat, to run back to my room. I can't handle the sensual curl of his lips or the sexy way the candlelight flickers against his skin.

However, I don't retreat. Ever.

And I'm not going to start now.

"I think maybe I could make you say it. Scream it, even," he whispers. His eyes are glued to my lips, and he's still, like he's contemplating whether to pounce, or run.

He's giving me a chance to go. To back down, to exit the room, and pretend this never happened. I recognize the opportunity for an exit when I see one.

I hesitate.

It has to be the wine.

It has to be the stress.

It has to be the fatigue.

It has to be the fact that I haven't slept with anyone since

Because from somewhere else in my mind, I hear myself say,

"Prove it."

CHAPTER 5

ALEXANDER

When Emma throws down the gauntlet, I waste no time.
One of my hands shoots out, gripping her neck. The other wraps around her hip, tugging her close to me. I knot my fingers lightly in her blonde hair, making sure that she can't escape me if she tried.

I want her to try.

She gasps when our lips meet, but one of her hands flies up and cups the back of my neck. I groan my approval, and I lick the seam of her lips with mine.

She opens for me.

"Good girl," I purr before I deepen our kiss.

Despite her prickly exterior, Emma is being a very, very good girl for me. Within seconds she's pressed up against my body. She's strong; I can feel that in the long lines of her arms, and the smooth press of her legs.

She's strong, sexy, and all mine.

I growl and lift her up, scooping my hands underneath her ass. She parts her legs, and I skim my hands up the sides of her hips, feeling the flex of her powerful thighs as she opens them wider so I can step between them.

God, she's sexy.

I press forward, pulling her slightly so that her legs dangle off the counter, and she's forced to wrap them around me for balance. I grind my hardness against her; she's hot and wet, and I want to be inside her.

I break our kiss, my lips tracing a path from her neck, down to her chest. I run my hands up her sides, lifting the edges of her shirt as I go.

When she pulls back, ducking so I can remove it, I tug it over her head without hesitating.

"Jesus, Emma," I breathe. Her perfect breasts, each a handful topped by a delectable pink nipple, glisten in the candlelight.

She looks away slightly. "My bra was wet."

"Thank god I didn't know earlier, or I would have ripped this off of you as soon as I could."

She arches into my hands as I cup her perfect handfuls. I lean forward, my lips hesitating over one stiff peak.

"Tell me to stop," I whisper.

She arches into my mouth instead.

I fasten on to one nipple, tugging at it. Emma pants, her fingers scraping against my scalp as she presses me closer.

"So eager for me, Emma," I smile as I lap at the other nipple.

"Shut up," she snaps.

I pull back. I grip her neck, hard, and smash our lips together.

It's a punishing kiss.

She moans into my mouth, clearly enjoying it.

When I pull back, her eyes look glossy. Her chest is flushed, and her little nipples pout at me.

I want her.

"Emma," I whisper. "If you want to stop, you have to tell me."

For a moment, I see the idea flash in front of her. She considers it, clearly thinking of it.

Then her eyes glitter, and she smiles.

"You haven't made me say your name yet," she whispers.

I growl, and I descend on her.

My hands pull the soft athletic leggings down off of her muscular legs. She kicks them off, and I'm pleased to discover that she wore panties to match her bra.

That is, she has neither one on.

I kneel in front of the kitchen island. I throw one of her smooth legs over one of my shoulders, then the other. Moving forward, I line my lips up with her heated core.

One long lick, and we both moan.

"You taste so good, Emma darling," I whisper against her slickness.

She only moans, pressing her heels into my back, urging me forward.

"Good girl," I whisper.

I oblige her.

My tongue works her slick seam, moving from the button that's the center of her pleasure back down to press inside her core. I bring my fingers up, pressing first one, then two inside her. I pump them slowly, lapping at the moisture that's evidence of her arousal as she bucks her hips against my mouth.

"You're so wet for me, Emma darling," I murmur as I press a kiss to the inside of her thigh. I glance up at her, and the sight is so erotic, I nearly come just watching her.

She's arched back, her hips thrusting against my mouth, her head tilted toward the ceiling. Her breasts are shuddering with each breath, and her smooth stomach flexes as she twitches her hips.

She's perfect.

I press my fingers upward, curling them to hit the spot that I know will make her lose her mind. "Are you ready to come for me, good girl?"

She pants in response.

I return to my task. I lick her clit, moving in strong, big circles. My fingers press inside her, probing and pulsing, until I feel the spot that sets her off like a bomb.

The taste of her orgasm on my lips is finer than anything I've ever experienced.

She screams. Her inner muscles pulse and flutter around my fingers, and her eyes close in ecstasy. She trembles, and I lick the last remnants of her pleasure as I pull my fingers back.

I gather her in my arms. She leans forward, her legs loosely wrapping around me as I stand and move her to the couch.

Gently, I deposit her down onto it. Her hair is wild, a torrent of blonde that spreads across the expensive-looking couch in a luxurious waterfall. She blinks sleepily back up at me, and I smile down at her.

I hope she's not done yet.

Because I haven't had nearly my fill.

I shed my pants, hopeful she's interested in what I have to offer. She stares at me, and I make sure I have her full attention when I ask.

"Ready for round two, Emma darling?"

In response, she smiles.

And her nod is all I need.

CHAPTER 6

EMMA

In the candlelight, Alexander looks like a god.

The living room is close enough to the kitchen that the flickering light of the emergency candles caresses his golden skin, a loving glimmer that makes the hard planes of his body look like they're crafted from something mortals can only dream of.

I should be worried about this.

Warning bells should be ringing in my mind.

But they're strangely silent.

Instead, I'm wrapped up in the moment. In the way his body moves over mine. The way his lips cover mine, the way his hands skate over my skin, teasing and touching and driving me toward oblivion.

I am never impulsive.

I never lose myself.

But it feels so good, I don't care at all that this is something I never do.

Quite the opposite, actually.

I'm reveling in it.

The orgasm that shattered me earlier still feels like it's pumping through my veins. I'm drunk with it; that and the wine make me feel like I'm on a different plane of existence.

I'm totally naked in front of Alexander Knight.

And he's looking at me like I'm the most beautiful woman he's ever seen.

His hands caress my legs, squeezing and kneading. His fingertips glide over me like he's trying to memorize every curve and dip of my body. The way he touches me feels reverent; it's almost like he's worshipping me.

It's a far cry from the alpha asshole doctor I see on a daily basis.

I won't lie; I absolutely love what he's doing to me.

I feel self-conscious about the stretch marks from where I carried Lily for no more than a second; he doesn't seem to care about them at all. His hands linger over two scars; one is from a knife wound, and the other a bullet hole from my last deployment.

"So tough," he murmurs. "Did you give them hell right back, beautiful Emma?"

I grin. "I did."

His answering smile makes my heart expand. "That's my girl."

I pretend that it doesn't make me giddy to hear him say 'my girl'. I'm not his girl. I'm not Alexander Knight's anything. I'm his employee. His flight nurse.

Nothing else.

But it is nice, just for a second, to pretend.

I widen my legs. "I want you," I purr.

His smile goes from proud to feral in mere moments. "Good," he murmurs. I don't know when he took off his pants, but when he stood up on his knees, I let my eyes wander.

They snag on his thick erection, which he's casually pumping with one hand while he surveys me.

Earlier, I felt all of that hardness pressed against me.

Now, I'm ready to feel him again.

"Say my name, and it's yours, Emma," he says darkly.

A thrill courses through my body.

It's a game? Let's play, Dr. Knight.

"Dr. Knight," I say in what I hope is a sultry voice. I let one of my hands drift down, until it presses against my clit. I start to play with myself, rubbing circles against my sensitive mound. "More," I whisper.

He growls. The hand on his cock moves faster, and my body responds with a rush of moisture.

"Alexander," he grunts. "Say it."

"Hmm," I look away.

It's a mistake.

Seconds later, he's pressed against me. His hand is on my throat, his fingers on my jaw. He forces me to look at him, controlling my face with his strong hands.

Normally, I'd hate being controlled like this.

However, given that he was just touching me like I was glass mere moments before, I think the gesture is… kind of sexy.

"Alexander," he grunts, staring into my eyes.

Oh, we're still playing. "Dr. Knight," I parry.

He growls, leans forward, and bites where my neck and shoulder meet.

It's pain that sends a cascade of pleasure over my skin. I moan and open my legs wider, my hips twisting and writhing as I try to get him closer. I want that thick cock between my legs. I want it rubbing against me.

I want it inside me.

As if he hears my thoughts, he rears back. His erection rubs against the seam of my lips, and we both groan as he coats himself in my moisture.

"Say my name, Emma, and I'll give you everything you want," he grunts.

I contort my body, seeking the contact with him. "Just give it to me," I moan.

"Say it," he snaps.

"Please," I murmur.

Surely, begging is going to get me somewhere.

All it earns me is another punishing kiss that leaves me breathless. This time, however, he puts his hand on my breast.

And when he rolls my nipple between his fingers, it's like a switch flips in my body.

Screw the game.

"Alexander," I whine, nearly mindless as I work myself against him. "Please."

When I feel the thick head of him press against my opening, I want to scream with joy.

"Good girl Emma," he says in that low, sexy tone. I moan in response. Who would have thought that I had such a praise kink?

"You're doing so good," he murmurs as he presses inside me further. "It wasn't so hard to say my name, now was it?"

That better be a rhetorical question.

Because with every inch he presses forward, words become more and more difficult to form.

When he's about halfway in, he freezes. "I don't have a condom," he barks.

Screw that as well.

"I have an implant," I moan. "I'm clean."

There's literally no way to verify that in the moment, but he nods. "Me too."

I trust him.

I have no option other than to trust him.

Because I want this so badly, I'd do anything to have it.

He presses further. His cock is thick and long, much bigger than my ex-husband's. I squeeze my eyes against the intrusion. It's almost too much, and I pant against the stretch of him.

"You take me so good, Emma. You're doing such a good job. Almost there. Look how pretty you are where you take me," he whispers.

I look down.

The sight of him disappearing into me is electric. I groan as moisture rushes out of me.

"God, Emma," he pants. "You're so sexy."

Looking at him sliding in and out of me, I feel it.

"Now that you've said my name, baby, let's see if I can make you scream it."

He starts to move rapidly. His lower abs flex as he pulses, the movements controlled, pistoning in and out of me.

I want to see him lose that iron control. I want to see him as wild for me as I am for him.

I arch, meeting him at each of his thrusts. I wrap my legs around his back, slamming myself against him as he moves down.

I drag my nails against his back, and when I lean up, I bite him lightly on the chest.

"Fuck, Emma," his voice is more guttural. I lean back down and press my fingers down against my clit, rubbing as he punches in and out of me.

"I'm close," I whisper again.

It's not a lie.

I'm about to come. Again.

I press harder, moving my fingers rapidly. Alexander looks down, watching me play with myself as he slides himself in and out.

"Come for me again, Emma darling," he grunts.

I obey.

And this time, I don't just say his name.

I scream it.

My eyes are closed, and my head is thrown back. Every muscle in my body tenses, and I literally see stars behind my eyelids. It's the most jaw-dropping orgasm I've ever had, and I feel like I've left my body entirely as it pulses through my skin.

Vaguely, I'm aware of Alexander's movements growing erratic. He pulses, grunting, and I hear something through my orgasmic haze.

Emma, I hear him whisper.

When he collapses over me, carefully making sure he doesn't crush me with his arms, I smile.

Looks like you're not the only one who can make someone say their name, Alexander Knight.

Gently, he presses a kiss to my forehead. "Stay here," he murmurs.

He slides out of me, and I linger, eyes closed. I feel heavy; my limbs are tired, my eyelids droop.

I'm satisfied. Perfectly, completely satisfied.

He returns; I feel the couch dip with his weight. I feel a warm towel between my legs, and he gently cleans the fluids from our combined lovemaking. It's a gesture that's a little awkward, but also very kind. With my ex, he always expected me to take care of myself. I have to use the bathroom still, but the fact Alexander thought of cleaning me up feels… nice.

Then, the towel is gone, and he's tucking me against his side.

"Sleep," he breathes into my ear. "The storm's still going. Power's still out. Might as well rest while we can."

I grin, and I snuggle into him.

As I drift off, I notice that in my mind, I haven't called him Dr. Knight in a while.

But I've definitely started to think of him as Alexander.

I'm not sure what the shift means.

But I do know that I'm not sure I can go back.

I wake, not to the storm, but to the chaotic buzzing of my phone.

I frown and look at it. My phone is almost dead, but my mom's name flashes on the screen. I pick it up. "Hello?"

"Em," my mom's voice is frantic. "Can you come home?"

My heart sinks. "Why? What's wrong?"

"It's Troy. He came by the house. He's out on the lawn, screaming," she says in a shaking tone.

"Call the cops," I gasp.

"I did. With the storm, they're going to take a while."

"Are you okay? Is Lily okay?"

"We're fine," my mom reassures me. "He hasn't come in. But he's yelling and Lily is scared."

"Mom, I…" I look down.

The phone is dead.

I can't help it. Tears flood my eyes, and I suck in a breath, fighting a sob.

I need to get to her.

My ex-husband, Troy Ververs, is not only an asshole.

He's a stalker as well.

We've moved twice, but it's no use.

Apparently, he found us again.

And I'm stuck here. In the Hamptons.

In a hurricane.

"Emma," Alexander's voice is surprisingly soft. "Are you okay?"

"Is your phone charged?" I ask.

He holds it up. "Died an hour ago."

My heart sinks. "I have… I need to get to Lily," I murmur frantically.

"Who is Lily?" he asks softly.

I'm so thrown off by the quiet, gentle tone of his voice, I answer without thinking about hiding her.

"She's my daughter."

Alexander frowns, then pulls me to him. He takes a deep breath. "Do you trust me?"

I peer up at him. "What?"

"Do you trust me?"

It's on the tip of my tongue to ask for more context. To understand more about what he means by "trust".

I'm surprised then when only one word comes out.

"Yes."

CHAPTER 7

ALEXANDER

I'm sure the storm has gone down in intensity.

Sightly.

It's still raining. The wind is still there.

But as I look at the weather and make an assessment, I know that this is the right choice to make.

Somehow, Emma's trust in me empowers me. It makes me feel important, and like I'm taking on something important.

Something bigger than myself.

I fire up the helicopter, and the rotor begins to spin. I shoot a glance at Emma, who is quietly gripping the arm of the seat.

Her knuckles are white.

I grit my teeth and look back at the helicopter's controls.

This machine is solid. It's state-of-the-art. It's big and stable and has a rating to fly through weather most helicopters wouldn't dream of.

That still doesn't mean it can take off in a hurricane.

"Here we go," I say through the headset to Emma.

She nods.

I press the controls, and the machine rises.

For a minute, it's sketchy. The rain batters us and the wind rips at the body of the chopper. Even I am sweating as we rise up through the storm.

We have to get to Emma's daughter, however.

At some point, I reach out and offer her my hand. "She's going to be okay," I say through the headset."

She nods and takes my hand. Her palm is so small in mine, and I curl my fingers around hers protectively.

She doesn't move it for the rest of the ride. She calls out directions, and eventually, the lights of New Haven break the horizon.

It's a miracle.

We drop down in a light drizzle, in the front yard of a very standard-looking neighborhood in New Haven.

Emma's out before I'm even close to shutting down the engine. She sprints to the house, opening the door before I can shout anything at her.

There's no sign of anyone around; the ex is clearly long gone. I peer through the sheets of rain at the street.

It's a quiet neighborhood.

The kind you see in movies; this is where kids grow up and play in the street, where there are holiday gatherings between neighbors.

It's a wholesome place.

Normally, it would make my skin crawl. I'm not a wholesome man; I haven't built my life to be oriented toward anything like that.

However, as I look around, I find that I'm less disgusted by the idea than I would normally be.

If this is what Emma expects from her future, then I could see why. It's definitely comfortable, it's absolutely safe, and it seems…

Charming.

Yes, I decide. Definitely charming.

Not at all cloying or overwhelming, as I had once thought I would feel if confronted with such a Rockwellian scene.

Interesting.

The chopper is finally ready to be disengaged. I turn everything off, then follow Emma into the house.

She left the door open. I cautiously push it open, then close it behind me.

Emma has her arms wrapped around a pale-looking little girl, and there's an older woman behind them both. Both Emma and the girl are sobbing; the older woman looks like she's been through hell and back.

"I was so worried," I hear Emma whisper.

The girl squeezes her mom tighter. "He was scary, mommy," she whispers back.

Who the hell would do this to a little girl? I growl thinking of what kind of sicko would scare his own child like this.

The noise is, apparently, audible.

Both Emma and her daughter look up.

Emma stands. Her arms come to rest on the little girl's shoulders. "Dr. Knight," she says softly.

My eye twitches at the formal address.

"This is Lily," Emma continues. Lily waves.

Cautiously, I wave back.

"Lily," Emma looks at her daughter, and warmth fills her gaze. "This is Dr. Knight. He's my boss."

"Did you fly the chopper?" she asks, her eyes round with wonder.

I laugh. Of course, a flight nurse's kid would call it a chopper. "Yes, I did."

"Will you stay in case my Daddy comes back?"

I'm frozen by her plea.

She's clearly terrified.

"Of course," I say confidently. "Nobody is going to bother you while I'm around."

Lily looks relieved.

Emma, however, frowns. "He has to go back to his own house, Lily bean," she says gently.

"Nonsense," the other woman sticks out a hand. "I'm Margaret. Welcome to my home. Stay as long as you like, Dr. Knight."

I step forward and shake her hand. "Pleasure to meet you. Thanks."

"Dr. Knight doesn't have time, Mom. He can…"

"The only place that I need to be is here," I firmly tell Emma. I raise an eyebrow to let her know I'm daring her to turn me down again.

Emma turns pink, but she shuts her mouth. "Let's get you to bed," she says to her daughter.

Lily nods happily and takes her mom's hand.

Margaret watches them go, then turns back to me. "Tea, Dr. Knight?"

"I'd love some."

It doesn't take long for Emma to come back.

That's a good thing. Margaret and I have reached a tentative truce, but it's nothing I'd call comforting. She's eyeing me with interest over a cup of tea when Emma returns to the kitchen.

"Mom," she says, "why don't you…"

"I'm going to bed," her mom interrupts. She abandons her tea and pauses in the doorway, looking back at us. "I'm a very heavy sleeper. In case you were interested," she says pointedly before walking away.

If the situation were different, I'd laugh.

Emma blows out a breath, picking up her mom's cup. She takes a sip and grimaces. "She always wants the weirdest herbal teas."

I dump mine in the sink. "Noted."

Emma blows on hers again, not meeting my eyes.

"So," I prompt. "What's up with baby daddy?"

"He's not…" she sighs. Shakes her head. "Do you care?"

I'm pinned by the question.

"Of course I care. I flew you back to your home in a hurricane, Emma. Obviously, I wouldn't have done that if I didn't care."

"Okay. Fair. I just… You're…why are you being nice to me?"

"I'm a nice guy," I say evenly.

Emma barks a laugh. "No. Really."

Really.

I wonder if either of us is ready for what that means.

I breathe in deeply, then out again.

Am I ready to tell her what I've noticed? What I've been fighting, that this weekend has painfully called to life?

Nope.

I'm not ready.

"You're my best nurse," I say instead.

Emma searches my face, then nods. She turns away.

I have a feeling that was the wrong answer.

"He's my ex-husband. We split up about two years ago."

"The same time you started working for me," I nod.

She shrugs. "Sure. He's not... he wasn't always like this. Lily and I left; he said he wouldn't follow."

"He did." It's not a question.

"He did," she agrees. She sighs. "But that's okay. I'll get the restraining order again. Lily and I can move..."

"Move?" I cut her off. The word fills me with anxiety.

Emma nods. "Yeah. It buys us some time. We've done this twice now. Moving in with my mom wasn't the best idea, but my last job didn't pay hardly anything. I've got enough saved up now that we can go somewhere. More remote, I think. Then it might take him longer to find us."

Move.

Remote.

Gone.

The words make my throat tighten.

If she moves, I won't see her every day.

I won't tease her.

I won't get to see the blush rise in her cheeks.

I won't get to see her spark with anger as she glares at me.

Move?

Hell no.

"No," I growl.

Emma looks up. "Excuse me?"

"No," I repeat. "You can't go anywhere."

"You're my boss, Dr. Knight. Not my dad," her voice rises, and her hands move to her hips.

I slam the door in a huff.

Outside, I pace back and forth in front of my helicopter.

The rain increases, and with it, the temperature drops.

Soon, my temper has cooled with the weather.

I realize two things.

One, I just did a terrible job inside. I need to tell Emma how I feel, even if I don't want to reveal that. It's scary, sure.

But since when have I ever run away from something because it scares me?

Two, I need to tell her.

And I know just the way.

CHAPTER 8

EMMA

When I get to work the next day, it's quiet.
Weirdly quiet.
"Hello?" I call out as I walk in.
Nobody answers me. The lights are off; even the heating system seems down.

I frown. The hurricane did some damage, but not like this.

"Is anyone here?" I call out to the empty building.

"I'm in here," a voice resonates from the main office.

I gulp.

It's Dr. Knight.

Alexander.

Heart in my throat, I wander into the office. The office is mostly dark. He's been sitting here alone, with the lights off, for God knows how long. His hands are flat, palms down, on the desk. Two papers sit on the desk in front of him.

My heart rate skyrockets. *What the hell is this?*

"Sit," he commands.

I want to resist, but I don't.

I sit.

"What are you doing?" I whisper.

He takes a deep breath. "Emma, you're fired."

"Are you freaking kidding me!" I screech, leaping out of the seat. "You're firing me because I slept with you?"

"Sit," he orders again.

"No," I hiss. "I won't sit. You can be a real jerk, but this is a jerk move even for you. I can't believe…"

"*Emma*," he interrupts me. "Sit."

There's something serious in his tone, and it catches my attention. I sit.

"You're fired," he continues. I bristle but he holds up a hand. "Because I have a proposition for you."

I blink. "What?"

He looks at the papers. "This document—" he indicates the one next to his left hand "—is a cash offer. It's no-strings attached; you can read it if you want, but I assure you, it's ironclad."

"Cash offer?"

He pushes it forward, and my eyes widen at the number of zeros at the top. "Dr. Knight…"

"It would give you the ability to run from your ex-husband. Forever. With all of the resources I can possibly give you, should you need them."

"Okay…" I prompt. I'm still not quite sure what's going on.

But I know that whatever it is, there's more to the story.

He pushes the second paper forward. "This one is something else."

I frown.

The page is blank.

"There's nothing on here," I look back up.

His green eyes glitter. "That one isn't written yet."

"Why not?"

"Because that option, Emma, is me."

I blink. "What does that mean?"

"It means, Emma Lowe, that should you choose this option, we make it together."

I'm still not understanding, but my heart pounds at his words. "What are you saying, Alexander?"

He smiles at my use of his name.

"Emma, you're an incredible woman. I've known you for a few years, and while I know I haven't always been the kindest, I want you to know that you are one hell of a woman. You're smart. You're incredibly resilient. You're strong beyond measure. You have my respect, and you're sexy as hell to boot."

I blush. "Alexander…"

"I want you. I want us. I want to try this out. I want to wake up to you and fall asleep together. I want to have a role in Lily's life, and mostly, I don't want you to live in fear. Ever again. In your life."

I can't believe my ears. I'm speechless; my lips move, but nothing comes out.

He moves from behind the desk, and he grabs my hand. "I want to try and see where things go with you, Emma. You are the only woman I've ever met who keeps me interested from dawn to dusk, and I'd be an idiot if I walked away from at least trying to do this with you."

"I… I don't know what to say…" I stammer.

He smiles and grabs the papers. "Don't say anything. Just choose."

I look between them. My eyes go from one paper to the next, looking at the block of text, then back at the blank page.

I close my eyes and look into my heart.

For a moment, I breathe deeply.

Then I open them, and smile.

And I reach for the blank page.

CHAPTER 9

ALEXANDER

Years have passed since that fateful evening when our paths crossed in the eye of a hurricane. The city that never sleeps had witnessed the transformation of our lives, of a love that defied the boundaries of time and circumstance.

Emma and I had embarked on a journey that transcended the walls of my office, a journey that led us to discover the profound depths of our hearts. Our love has flourished, like a resilient flower pushing through the cracks of the concrete jungle.

As the years unfolded, Emma's strength and resilience remain unwavering. She has blossomed into a woman of indomitable spirit, her sassy demeanor a testament to her enduring spirit. Her daughter, Lily, who had once been a shy observer in our story, has grown into a vibrant, confident young woman. She has become a daughter to me in every sense, and I love being her father.

Our journey had not been without its trials. We have faced our fair share of challenges, navigating the complexities of blending our lives and healing the scars of our pasts. But with unwavering support, trust, and love, we had overcome each obstacle that came our way.

"Hey. Are you ready for dinner?" Emma asks.

My eyes drift over to her and Lily. They're unloading the groceries to our very own house in the Hamptons, ready for a long weekend away together.

My ring glimmers on Emma's hand. She wanted something small and discrete, of course.

But that's not exactly my style, so a two-carat diamond, and several stacks of diamond bands, wink at me from her fingers.

As I look at Emma and Lily, my heart swells with gratitude for the chance encounter that had brought us together. Our love story has unfolded in the most unexpected of ways, proving that destiny had a way of guiding two souls towards their happily ever after. With the promise of a future filled with love, laughter, and endless possibilities, we embrace the beautiful tapestry of our lives, forever grateful for the love that has blossomed beyond the office, beyond the city, and into our hearts.

About Sophie Thurn

Sophie Thurn is an emerging voice in contemporary romance, blending the poignant intricacies of the human heart with the complex world of professional life. Known for her emotionally rich storytelling and her knack for capturing love stories that blossom in the least expected places, Thurn's novels resonate with the silent yearnings of the heart while reflecting on the daily boundaries we navigate.

Inspired by the rhythmic ebb and flow of her coastal hometown's tides, her narratives mirror the tumultuous journey of love. Having spent years in the corporate world, her writing is imbued with authenticity, drawing on personal experiences and the vibrant tales of those she's encountered.

With a reverence for classic literature and an appreciation for fine wine and well-brewed coffee, Thurn's prose dances between classical elegance and contemporary challenges. When not immersed in writing or ensnared in her garden's complexities, she enjoys seaside strolls with her rescue dog, Jasper, musing on the next great love story to tell.

Sophie Thurn offers a look into a realm where propriety and passion collide, and each story is a testament to the irresistible dance between concealing and revealing our deepest desires.

Contact us:

Website: sophiethurn.com

Email: info@sophiethurn.com

Thanks for reading.

Get a sneak peek into the forthcoming book with this exclusive preview!

Healing Hearts

An Office Romance Sequel- Preview

Coming Soon

"**H**ealing Hearts: An Office Romance**" by Sophie Thurn is an entrancing novel that artfully intertwines the complexities of professional ethics with the unpredictable nature of the human heart. Set against the backdrop of a bustling counseling center, this story delicately explores the evolving relationship between Mia, a talented therapist, and Daniel, her charismatic mentor and superior. Their journey begins with an unexpected proposition—a seemingly innocent invitation to a charity ball that sets the stage for a deeply emotional and ethically challenging romance.

Mia has always been a paragon of professionalism, understanding the critical importance of maintaining boundaries in her work. However, the arrival of Daniel, an experienced and charming therapist, introduces a whirlwind of emotions that Mia finds increasingly difficult to compartmentalize. The plot thickens as they find themselves at a crossroads, where the lines between personal feelings and professional responsibilities become blurred.

The narrative takes the reader through the highs and lows of their relationship, marked by clandestine meetings, unspoken desires, and the palpable tension of a forbidden love. As the story progresses, it delves into the moral dilemmas they face, from the fear of jeopardizing their careers to the guilt of potentially crossing ethical lines. Their connection deepens with every secret rendezvous, challenging not only their professional integrity but also their personal beliefs about love, loyalty, and sacrifice.

Sophie Thurn masterfully crafts a narrative that is both compelling and thought-provoking, inviting the reader to question the boundaries of love and duty. Her characters are richly developed, each grappling with their own inner conflicts and desires, making them relatable and deeply human. The novel is filled with moments of intense emotion, from heart-wrenching uncertainty to moments of pure, unadulterated joy, capturing the essence of a complicated yet passionate relationship.

As the story unfolds, Mia and Daniel must navigate the consequences of their actions, facing both internal and external challenges. Their journey is one of self-discovery, courage, and the power of love to transcend conventional boundaries. The narrative builds to a climax that leaves the reader eager for more, yet satisfied with the depth and resolution of the story.

"Healing Hearts: An Office Romance" is a gripping and emotionally charged novel that promises to be a memorable read. It is ideal for those who enjoy contemporary romance with a twist of ethical complexity, offering a unique perspective on the struggles and triumphs of love in the modern world. This book is a testament to the enduring power of love and the human capacity for change, making it a must-read for fans of sophisticated and emotionally rich storytelling.

Made in the USA
Columbia, SC
16 December 2024

49596553R00028